BIGFAT

Christmas

Hedonist

Hedonist

CONTENTS

BIG FAT CHRISTMAS

Ever since I moved into my new flat, I've been obsessed with my neighbour to the right. Every time I leave my front door, I hope to bump into him. And whenever I'm at home, I wonder what he's up to in the apartment right next door to me.

I don't see too much of him, but he's managed to push all my buttons. 'Fat' doesn't quite describe him appropriately; he's huge. Tall and broad enough to fill up the whole hallway when he walks by. With a kind and handsome face and gentle brown eyes that I could spend a lifetime losing myself in. He has a sadness hanging around him, though. Perhaps that's what fascinates me most. He's a tragic mystery, just begging to be unravelled.

Karen - the middle-aged woman who lives to my left - didn't have a kind word to say about him when I first asked, though. She called him a loser. A drunk. Perhaps even a junkie. She finished her rant with the complaint that despite telling the landlord numerous times that he has working girls over sometimes; nothing has been done about it.

Karen seems like a whiner generally, so I figured she must be exaggerating or mistaken entirely. I'd already decided: Eric could do no wrong in my mind.

I still can't reconcile what she told me with my first impressions of the rather shy man whom I'd nervously said hello to in the elevator. Karen's wild insinuations about booze, drugs and prostitutes don't fit.

Sure, I've regularly seen him carry his groceries up, and the recycling down. And most of the time he has way more bottles on him than a single person living alone should. It concerns me, but what business is it of mine? I'm not his mom.

I'm just a girl, quietly wondering whether he even remembers my name. Or if he thinks about me even half as often as I do about him.

In any case, our interactions are always civil and even include a bit of small talk. I've already learned that he's a freelancer and that he inherited the lease from his mother when she passed a couple of years ago. My own observations concluded that he leaves the house a handful of times a week at the most, just to go to the shops. He never has friends or family over as far as I can tell and doesn't interact with any neighbour other than me. He seems to live a lonely, isolated sort of life. A far cry from the party animal Karen described to me.

I often wonder if I should reach out more. *Really try to* get to know him. And I've always been too much of a chicken shit to follow through.

But that's about to change.

Today, on the 23rd of December, late afternoon, I'm busying myself in the kitchen as usual. As a food blogger, the kitchen is basically my office most of the time. Trying out recipes, plating them up and taking photographs on a carefully staged dining table. That's my life.

I'm just finishing up after a holiday themed shoot for the blog, when I hear a noisy exchange out in the hallway. My curiosity is piqued, so I open the door just wide enough to observe.

Karen from next door is getting into it with a young girl in a short fur coat, fishnet tights and shoes that can only be described as *stripper heels*.

"We don't need the likes of you coming here, cheapening the place up. Tell that filthy John of yours that I'm going to call the police if it happens again!" Karen shouts.

I hold my breath to hear more, but a loud thud signals her departure. The girl shrugs and carries on walking towards the elevator. Though I hardly know the man she inevitably must have been visiting, a pang of jealousy hits me. So, perhaps Karen was right all along? And if that's the case, do I really want to get any closer to him?

Still, I can't quite get my nosiness under control. I rush out into the hallway, with a half-baked plan already formed in my head. Finally, I catch her in front of the elevator moments before it's due to arrive.

"Hey," I call out.

The girl turns and folds her arms.

"I know. You guys will call the police. Your friend already told me."

I shake my head. "No, that's not it and she isn't my friend. I was wondering if you were hungry?"

She frowns and pauses for a moment. "The fuck do you mean?"

"Look, I've been trying all these recipes for my food blog, and I've got this mountain of Christmas food at my place and no one to give it to. Carry some home with you, if you want. I just don't know what to do with it all." I smile at her.

Luring strangers into my house with food; classy, right?

She stares at me for a couple of seconds, then reciprocates my smile.

"Yeah, okay! That's very kind of you."

I walk back to my place, and the girl follows. So far, so good. Once in my kitchen, I point it all out to her and grab some disposable containers from one of the overhead cabinets.

"Here. Take whatever you'd like. I've got roast turkey, of course, gravy, veggies, mashed potato… you get the idea."

She eagerly helps herself while I stand back and watch. My curiosity is killing me, so I finally initiate the conversation I'd wanted to have all along. The whole reason for approaching her in the first place.

"You were visiting my neighbour, right?" I ask.

She gives me a suspicious side-eye. "Eric, yeah."

"You guys know each other well?"

She puts the serving spoon down and turns to face me head-on. "What's it to you?"

I raise both my hands in a defensive sort of pose. "Look, it's none of my business. I was actually just wondering if I should ask him if he wants some of this stuff too. I don't know what his plans might be for the holidays though."

It seems like a good enough justification for sticking my nose where it doesn't belong. Maybe.

Still, she has her head cocked to the side in a defensive sort of stance. "He's lonely, you know. He calls me over maybe once a month, but it's not what you think."

"It's *none* of my business," I confirm.

"All he wants to do is sit on the couch and watch telly. Sometimes we talk a little, but he's not the chatty type." She smiles briefly and looks away again.

"Really?" I can feel my eyes widen, even if I'm trying my best not to sound too eager.

"He literally pays me just to sit there with him. At most, I'll hold his hand or something." The girl chuckles. "If that other neighbour of yours wants to call the police on us, they're not going to find anything worth arresting someone over. His calls are always a nice change of pace for me."

I don't know whether to laugh or cry. He pays an escort to watch TV with him. Shit, I'd do that for free...

"So, you think I should ask, then?"

"I'm sure he'd be thrilled if you do." She grins at me and holds up the two full containers. "Well, thanks for the food."

"You're welcome," I say, sporting an equally wide grin myself now.

I excitedly watch her leave, and I don't even know

why, really. If everything I've just learned about Eric is true, then I shouldn't even consider getting closer to him. Fucked up men are my kryptonite.

I ought to run the other way before I end up tangled up in a mess that's too big for me to manage. Of course, I'd never follow my own advice, no matter how sensible it is.

Eric:

Leslie left at five, and as usual, her departure leaves behind a gaping hole in my chest. It's not that I love her; that would be silly. But when she comes over, life almost feels normal for a little while. *Almost.*

I feel a little bit less like a loser, and more like a regular person who has others in his life who care. She might only visit me because I'm paying her, but that's still better than nothing at all.

Now, though, the moment has passed. Nobody cares anymore and the silence of my empty living room is deafening. All I can do is think about those things other people take for granted, which I'll never have.

Friendship. Companionship. Love...

The only sound I do hear is Karen's shrill voice in the hallway, nagging as usual. I used to think nobody would care if I lived or died, but I've come to the conclusion that Karen will be thrilled once I kick the bucket. Perhaps one day soon, she'll get what she wants. Maybe that will be my Christmas gift to the world.

I crack open a fresh bottle and close my eyes as the fiery liquid passes through my throat. Once I force down half of it, I know the numbness will kick in and it won't hurt so much anymore. If I finish it off, I'll definitely black out, and the hours will pass by themselves. If I make it quick enough, perhaps it'll be over forever.

But I don't get the chance to drink more than those first couple of sips. A knock on my door interrupts the eerie quiet. I put the vodka back down and just listen for a second.

Is Karen coming to give *me* an earful now too? I thought she'd given up on trying to berate me in person ever since I slammed the door in her face last time. Perhaps she'll go away if I ignore her.

I take another sip and muffle a coughing fit. Shit, my throat's on fire.

"Hey, it's Paige, from next door," a voice much friendlier than Karen's announces herself. She knocks again. "Are you there?"

Just like that, my heart starts racing so fast, it makes my head spin. *Paige.* I try not to think about her too much, at least not while I'm still in my senses. But she always finds her way back into my thoughts when my defences are down.

Ever since she's moved in, I've felt utterly conflicted. On the one hand I find myself going out as often as I can just to catch a glimpse of her. That in itself is bizarre enough.

And on the other hand, I pray for the ground to swallow me up whenever she's around. Because her presence hurts.

She's beautiful as well as an all-round good person. The way she smiles at me when she says hello threatens to tear my heart in two. Because I know I'm not worthy of her attention. I don't deserve to breathe the same air she does. Or ride the same elevator.

I'm less than the dirt stuck on the bottom of her shoes, and yet she makes it a point to talk to me as an equal every time we bump into each other. And like an asshole, I have been trying to orchestrate a meeting every other day or so.

If it's been creeping her out, she certainly hasn't let it show.

She knocks for a third time, and although I know I'm in no state to deal with her right now, I still force myself into action. Like an addict, I can't resist catching a glimpse of the object of my fascination.

It isn't every day that a beautiful woman *voluntarily* comes to my place.

My knees ache furiously as I heave myself up on my final try and stumble towards the door.

"I'm here," I announce myself, then stifle further coughs as I unlock the door.

"Hi!" She greets me with a wide smile.

Fuck. I wish I could just vanish. "Hi."

I'm quite a bit taller than her, meaning that her face is roughly at chest-height. Not my best feature. But then again, I don't really have a *best feature*. It's all pretty much revolting.

"Umm… so…" she starts.

I sheepishly look down at myself and am disgusted

by what I see. My t-shirt is already straining uncomfortable over my huge belly, and I'd only ordered it a month back. What an embarrassment I am. A sad excuse for a man. No wonder she's lost for words.

"I don't know if I'd mentioned, but I've got a food blog, right?" she says.

"Right." *God, should I ask her in?* Offer her something to drink?

My place is too much of a shithole; I couldn't possibly subject Paige to any of this. Fresh tears sting in the corners of my eyes, and my chest is still on fire too.

"And I've just finished doing the photography for a few Christmas recipes this afternoon, and I couldn't possibly eat it all… I was wondering if you'd like to-"

I frown. What is she asking me, exactly? I try to breathe, but my throat tries to close up and I barely manage to cover my mouth before coughing some more.

"Oh dear, are you alright?" she asks, resting her hand on my upper arm.

I still can't breathe, but try to nod in reassurance. Her touch doesn't help; it almost singes my skin with its intensity, and I panic some more.

But just like that, she's gone. Light-headedness sets in, requiring me to steady myself against the door frame and give it one last try to clear my airways. Now I've done it. This was the first and only time Paige has ever come to my door. She was trying to strike up a conversation, and I scared her away. It's probably for the best, and yet I regret it anyway.

But then, out of nowhere, she reappears.

"Here," Paige says.

She hands me a small brown bottle and rests her hand on my arm again. "Cough syrup. One sip should do it."

Although her touch distracts me again, I do as I'm told. She's right. I'm relieved to breathe freely again.

"I'm sorry, I don't know what happened," I explain, while giving the bottle back to her.

"You keep it. This year's flu season is a bitch," she says. "I've been battling a sore throat for weeks as well."

I don't tell her that it probably wasn't the flu. It's probably the fact that my throat is raw from waking up severely hungover this morning, and then it got burned further by the cheap no label vodka I've chugged before and after Leslie's visit. *God, I truly am pathetic.*

She was asking me something, before I started making a spectacle of myself. But now, she's just staring at me silently, no doubt regretting she ever came by. I glance down at my arm, where her hand is still touching me. She pulls it away just as quickly as she realises what I'm looking at.

Paige is not just beautiful, she's radiant. Even right now in her track pants and cable-knit hoodie. Her elegant features and blue eyes remind me of a pretty porcelain doll. Fragile and precious. By far the most gorgeous woman I've ever laid eyes on. I could spend the rest of my life just staring at her.

Surely, I must be creeping her out now. Why did she come to *my* door, of all places?

"Actually, I'd wanted to check if you're busy," she speaks up again. "But maybe you should rest, huh? That cough sounds nasty."

I shake my head. "Not busy." And the only rest I had planned on getting is an alcohol induced coma.

"Then, maybe you'd like to have dinner? Seeing as I've got all this food just lying there in my kitchen. It would be a shame to waste it."

I can hardly believe my ears. She's inviting me to dinner. At her place.

The state I'm in, I wouldn't have asked me. I wouldn't have touched me either, or smiled at me the way she tends to. Am I imagining things now?

"Right now?" I ask.

She nods eagerly.

I ought to refuse her invitation; make some excuse and head back inside. But the way she's looking up at me with those big expectant eyes, I find myself answering 'yes' instead.

"Give me a minute, I'll be right there," I say.

She smiles again. As though she's genuinely happy I've accepted. Although I know that couldn't possibly be right, my heart feels like it's about to explode anyway. I close the door behind me and wonder if our conversation even really took place.

Paige:

I walk back across the hallway to my place with a spring in my step. The plan has worked. He's coming over!

The urge to tidy up overwhelms, but I stop myself.

It's a cosy sort of a mess in here; whereas his place was indeed a total disaster as Karen had warned. He wouldn't even notice the difference if I moved any of this stuff around.

Despite my excitement, the sensible part of my brain is still insisting that this is all a big mistake. I'm a sucker for a project. The sadness I saw in his eyes has hooked me in. And that's on top of what that girl told me.

He's lonely, just like me. He pays her - not for sex, but for the most basic form of companionship.

How on earth am I supposed to play it cool, knowing all that? My mind is saying run, but my heart is screaming at me to get closer. Maybe it's a motherly instinct thing? A very incestuous motherly instinct, if at all, because I know exactly where I want this thing to go and it isn't anywhere platonic. If he has any sense at all, he'll run for the hills before I sink my claws into him. Because as attracted as I was to him before, my desire has reached feverish levels now.

I hear a knock at *my* door now, wiping the last of my doubts away.

"It's open!" I call out. "I'm in the kitchen."

I've only just finished lining up the various dishes near the microwave to warm up later when I turn to find him standing there, awkwardly holding up a bottle of something brown with a black label.

"Housewarming gift," he says. "I'm sorry, it's all I had."

"Rum, huh? Just what I need for this Christmas Fruitcake recipe I've been planning to work on next." I grin at him. "Thank you!"

Just now, he was in a t-shirt. It had to have been at least a 5xl, and it was still rather tight. I only remember, because I'd mentally started taking it off him already. Now, he's wearing a hooded jacket on top of it, and it looks like he hurriedly combed his hair as well. He looks so cuddly, but I resist the urge to pounce.

The scent of cologne subtly fills in the air between us.

For someone who keeps to themselves and has a flat that looks like it's gearing up to appear on an episode of *Hoarders*, he always smells surprisingly nice. He's obviously a mess on the inside, but every time I've come across him, he's been well groomed. It's one of the first things I noticed about him. After I got over how absolutely immense he is.

"I'll make some tea to soothe that bad throat of yours, what do you say?" I suggest.

He agrees with a nod, prompting me to turn the kettle on.

When I turn again, I find him sheepishly looking around my place, before finally pausing on the large umbrella light set up by the dining table.

"Nice, umm... decor."

"Thanks... I have a lot of these props and things for my food photography. Half the time, this place looks more like a studio, than a home," I explain.

"Right."

A minute or so of silence later, I hand him a steaming mug of ginger tea with honey.

"It's an old home remedy; my mom always used to make it for me whenever I felt poorly," I comment. "Would you like to sit down?"

He glances at the dainty looking dining chairs and shakes his head. "I'm okay."

Realising that they do look a bit fragile for someone of his stature, I add: "Maybe we'll hang out in the living room?"

"Okay."

I follow him into the lounge. He makes my flat look so tiny, just by being here. I love it.

And now I'm also grateful for the humongous couch, which ordinarily looks so out of proportion with the rest of the furniture. It fits him perfectly, and I have to control myself not to cuddle up next to him right away. That would be weird, right? We barely even know each other. I mustn't get ahead of myself.

Instead, I pause for a moment and allow myself to just *feel* it. My work is solitary, and I've only just moved in last month, so I don't know too many people in the neighbourhood yet. Only him and Karen, and the latter I tend to avoid as much as possible.

It's nice having someone else around, even for a little while. Part of me understands why he pays for exactly that. Little does he realise I'd volunteer for that job in a heartbeat. Two lonely souls, living next door to each other. It's a match made in heaven, isn't it?

"I wasn't looking forward to Christmas this year," I remark.

"You don't like the holidays?" He looks up from his

tea. Colour is returning to his face; the sight makes me feel warm inside.

"I do, but I don't have any family in the area," I confess. "It's never fun celebrating alone…"

Eric:

When she tells me that she's been dreading the holidays, I'm almost speechless.

This amazingly attractive and kind woman has no one to celebrate Christmas with? How the hell does that happen? I want to ask her exactly that, but I'm too much of a coward.

"I haven't been looking forward to it either," I say instead.

"It was going to be just me, curled up on the couch with a pint of Rocky Road, watching all the *Die Hards* one after the other," she says.

Although I still feel like something died deep inside my chest, I can't suppress a smile. "Have you been reading my mind?"

"Why?"

"That's what *I* was going to do for Christmas," I say.

I don't even know where all this is coming from. The conversation is flowing somewhat comfortably, which is a miracle, considering how nervous she's made me every other time we've met. And now I find myself sharing a bit of banter with her.

"Well, great. Why don't we do that together, then?"

she suggests.

"It's a date." It slips out before I can stop myself. I swallow hard and wonder if I should backtrack. But instead of dwelling on the awkwardness of my statement, she sits down on the sofa next to me and folds her legs up underneath her to get comfortable.

"Okay, it's a date."

She purses her lips and blows into her mug of ginger tea before taking a first, careful sip.

It's insane to think that I'm here, sitting in Paige's apartment, only moments after having Leslie over. And I've already spoken more with Paige than I did in a whole hour with Leslie. Obviously, you don't invite call girls over to talk to them, usually, but it's not like I do anything else with her either.

I'm not that kind of guy. All I wanted was some company. I'm not interesting, or sociable, so I'm perfectly okay with the idea of having to pay someone to spend time with me. Actually no, that's not entirely true. I'm not okay with it. It kills me, but I don't have an option. The idea of having to go out into the world and actually befriend other people freaks me out.

Taking initiative in social situations does not come naturally to me. I would have never known Paige's name had she not introduced herself to me. Every exchange since has been initiated by her as well. It's a kindness most people don't bestow on me. But she does. Every single time we meet.

Just like this, right now. I'm here, because she took the first step. And I'm so very grateful for it. I wish I knew how to tell her without sounding like a complete loser.

"Hungry?" she asks, after putting her mug down on the coffee table.

"I could eat." I can always eat.

I *do* always eat, basically. It seems to make me less anxious, if only for a while. Though, the thought of her watching me eat is making me panic all over again.

She hands me the TV remote and her fingers brush past mine in the process, sending my thoughts racing. I want her. I want her so much; it's making my heart ache. So inappropriate. If she had any idea about how I feel, she'd throw me out of her place, and rightly so.

"Make yourself at home. I'll warm up dinner."

I'm breathless again, but this time it's not the cough, but her presence that causes it. She gets up and I track her as she leaves for the kitchen. I don't know what I've done to earn her charity, but she's made my year already.

Perhaps I should ask if she needs a hand. Be polite; act helpful. Anything, just to ensure this isn't the last time she invites me over.

But her sofa is low, and my knees are extremely stiff. I'm thoroughly sunken in and only now realising that I'm going to have real trouble getting up again. This isn't how I would have liked our first proper interaction to go; with me trapped in her furniture.

Panic washes over me, and my chest tightens again like it threatened to do earlier. I take a sip of tea, and try to focus on its soothing effect on my throat, but it's hopeless. All I can do is sit there, with my heartbeat in my throat, hoping this anxiety passes soon enough.

This is exactly why I lead the life I do. Because this sort of shit can happen without warning or notice. I'm hyperventilating, and I have no idea how to stop it before she comes back.

The thought of her seeing me like this only makes it worse.

Paige:

With the first dish heating up in the microwave, I pause for a moment, and inspect the various dinner plates in the cabinet. My crockery collection is hopelessly mismatched. I have one or two items in each design, enough to take a nice picture with, but not enough of one type for real-life company to join me for a meal. I decide on one of the bigger ones for him, and another in a similar colour for myself. It takes nearly ten minutes to warm up all the food.

Rather than serve him in the kitchen, I pile all the various dishes onto a large tray and carry everything into the living room. He's sure to have an appetite. No one of his size gets that way eating modest portions. Although I know it's weird, the thought that I'll get to watch him now pleases me and turns me on quite a bit.

I put it all down and glance over at him just as I'm about to start serving.

He's looking rather worse for wear. His face is pale again and he's even starting to sweat a little.

"Are you okay?" I ask.

"Yeah, great. Think that cough's back," he speaks in a choked voice.

Although he's trying to play it cool, his wheezy, shallow breaths and panicked look in his eyes aren't fooling me. I recognise this and it isn't a cold or a cough.

I leave the plates on the table and sit down next to him.

"You're freaking out a bit, aren't you?" I say.

He shakes his head, but his eyes continue to tell a different story.

"Has this happened before?" I ask.

"Yes."

I take his hand and thread my fingers through his. Although he's warm, his palms are clammy. His touch makes me nervous, but I try to focus on putting him at ease instead.

"Can you take a deep breath for me? Hold and count to five, then exhale slowly."

He closes his eyes and tries to do as I say. It takes him a few attempts to get it right once. Then, he exhales.

"It's going to be fine. This'll pass," I say, though I'm battling my own racing heart at the moment.

His eyes open briefly when I put my other hand on his shoulder, rubbing it encouragingly. He's so big. So fleshy. I wish we could skip past this awkwardness somehow. We're meant to be together, aren't we? We could have something beautiful, if only we got over the weirdness.

Almost simultaneously, his fingers tighten through mine. My heart skips a few beats as I forget to breathe myself.

He's gorgeous. How do I tell him how I feel without making things even weirder? Because I desperately want him. Always have, since I first laid eyes on him. And now he's in my flat, on my sofa; his hand in mine. This is a very slippery slope I find myself on.

But instead of taking things further right away, I continue to instruct him to breathe in deeply and hold it for a few seconds at a time. It takes a while, but finally his breaths slow to normal, and his expression calms.

"I'm sorry," he stammers. Now his formerly pale face is turning a bit red; he's obviously embarrassed.

I smile at him. "Don't worry about it. Glad you're okay now."

All I want to do is give him a hug and tell him not to worry about it. I'm certainly not judging him for what happened; the same shit has happened to me more times than I care to count.

I'm still leaning over him with one hand on his shoulder, and the other holding on to one of his. It feels natural -right- though my heart is still racing furiously. He's making no efforts to let go, and neither am I.

And for a change, he isn't avoiding eye contact with me either. Is he thinking about the same thing I am? Can he feel this same overwhelming attraction that I feel?

God, give me the strength to make the first move,

because there's no way he ever will.

I take a deep breath and lean down closer, then I brush my lips ever so gently against his, just to gauge his reaction. His hand reaches for the back of my neck, guiding me further down. My heart rejoices. This wasn't a mistake or miscalculation after all.

I don't know who opened their mouth first, him or me. We're both equally eager. Equally lost in the moment.

He shifts in his seat, as though he's trying to get up, but he's got nowhere to go.

I straddle him and find myself overwhelmed by his big strong arms as he draws me in closer. My legs are spread wide to fit around him, it actually makes my hamstrings burn a little. It's a sweet sort of a pain, though, because it means I'm close to getting what I really want.

Our tongues intertwine, and his hands keep me firmly in place, pressed up against his full frame. He's a great kisser. Enthusiastic, but not sloppy.

And his body, oh my God. He's utterly perfect. Soft. Squishy. Huge. And so very warm and inviting.

I moan into his lips when he shifts underneath me, causing his humongous belly to jiggle up against me. His rock-solid erection brushes past my crotch. God, I want him so badly. I have, ever since I first spotted him in the hallway outside my flat.

My sexy giant. Beautifully fucked up as he is, Eric pushes all my buttons.

Eager lips beg for all of my attention, but I pull back

just to get a better look at his face anyway.

"Jesus. Why?" he stammers. His eyes are half-shut, his cheeks are flush.

He's perfect. I cup his fat cheeks with both hands. What a gorgeous man he is.

I don't answer, except by kissing him more firmly this time. Hopefully that gets the message across loud and clear.

His arms twitch as they tighten around me further. My own find their way around his shoulders. I grind down once against the hard bulge between us. It presses up into my clit, making me tingle with anticipation. His entire body shudders and he lets out a raw groan into my lips.

Hardly anything has happened yet, but I realise he's already done, at least for the moment.

Even though I would have liked to tease him some more, I'm thrilled. The girl must have told the truth. There's no way he'd be this primed for release twenty minutes after screwing a hooker. Whatever he's got left to give, I'm determined to take it all tonight.

Eric:

It all happened so quickly.

Mere moments after feeling like I was going to die in Paige's living room, I find myself making out with her, and shooting a load into my boxers in the process.

She doesn't even stop to acknowledge my shame. Her hands are still on me, her lips pressed up against mine. Hot breaths tickle my face.

I don't know what I've done to deserve this. She's a vision of perfection, and the blind panic that had washed over me earlier is gone without a trace. In its place, there's a fresh load of embarrassment to accompany the damp patch developing on my crotch.

"I'm so sorry," I mumble into her mouth.

"For?" she asks.

I can't find the words for a sensible reply.

One of her hands creeps up the side of my belly. She's digging her fingers in, fondling and squishing me as though that's all she's been wanting to do to me all along. It feels kind of nice. No one has ever touched me like this, unless they were trying to mock my size. But she isn't laughing. She's looking down at me like she owns me instead and it fills me with pride.

"I don't know," I stammer.

She leans back; her shapely buttocks crush down hard on my spent cock. There is no way she did it unknowingly. No chance she didn't know exactly how horny I got the very second her lips touched mine.

Her expression is calm, almost zen-like. "This was all a bit sudden, but-" She bites her bottom lip and makes eye contact with me.

I nod. I can't quite contain my shock at how everything went down.

"I've been crushing on you for weeks now," she adds. "It's why I asked you over."

I don't know what to say. "Why on earth would you?"

She shrugs and smiles. "You're just so big and cuddly. Just my type! I can tell you, I'm so relieved. I might have died of embarrassment if you hadn't kissed me back just now."

Her words don't quite ring true, but I'm too distracted to question her immediately.

At some point during our feverish make out session, the zip of my hoodie ended up all the way down. The too-small t-shirt I'd tried to hide earlier has made a reappearance and I'm pretty sure it's ridden up quite a bit. I'm not sure whether to laugh or cry. Her hand is now resting on the bare skin the inadequate t-shirt has revealed. I so wish I could hide it all. Exchange this body for a better one that deserves to be here with her.

"You shouldn't concern yourself with me," I warn her. "I'm a mess."

"I figured."

Although she says that, her eyes are still staring at me like how I might look at a pint of Ben & Jerry's. Is this what lust looks like when you're on the receiving end of it? But, why? I sure as hell don't deserve it. She has no idea who I really am.

I place my hands on her upper arms and shake her gently to get her to focus again.

"Seriously. I'm disgusting. Everything I do all day is sit on my ass and eat. And when I'm done eating, I drink," I complain.

"Okay."

"And when I'm done drinking, if I'm not already passed out, I continue to sit there and feel sorry for myself, and then do it all over again."

She cups my face and glances down at my lips again. "And when you're done feeling sorry for yourself, occasionally you hire a call girl to give you company. Right?"

I'm speechless. She knows about Leslie. I mean, obviously she does. Karen made a huge scene when she was leaving, so Paige could have overheard it all, but I still kind of assumed that I'd been spared that particular shame. My dirty secret, exposed.

"Yeah. That too," I mumble.

"I'll watch TV with you for free, you know," she quips and purses her lips. "Anytime you want."

If she's joking, I can't tell. She looks pretty fucking serious. How the hell does she know that that's all I do with Leslie? Unless... *Oh fuck, they talked, didn't they?*

"And I'll make you dinner after, too."

I don't know what to say to that either.

"And once we're done with TV and dinner, I'll do a whole lot more if you'll have me," she adds in a breathy, sexy voice.

I feel like screaming, but I'm too breathless myself. "Why the fuck would you?" I ask instead.

"Because I want to." She shrugs.

"I nearly had a heart attack just now, because I realised I couldn't get up to help you in the kitchen," I confess. Just admitting it threatens to make me lose my nerve all over again.

"You had an anxiety attack. I used to get them too. It passed."

"You're missing the point. I'm such a fat fucking slob, my knees are killing me and I can't get up off this sofa right now," I complain.

She shrugs. "That's cool. I don't want you to get up."

"Look at me! I'm a fucking science experiment gone wrong!" I shout.

Those tears I'd fought back earlier when Leslie left, have made a reappearance. This time, there's no way to stop them or play it cool. God, I wish I'd had more than just those few sips of vodka I managed before her interruption. Perhaps then, I wouldn't feel quite so ashamed.

Why won't Paige listen to what I'm trying to say?

She cuddles into my arms, kisses the side of my neck, and my heart breaks further.

"I like how you look," she whispers. "And how you feel against me. And how you kissed me just now."

"There's no way," I say, mostly to myself.

Still, at least she hasn't commented on the stickiness developing between us. I've been saved from that particular humiliation for now.

"Most of all, I like how hard you got for me. It seems that all the stuff I like about you, you like about me too."

Her voice sends shivers down my spine. Maybe I did die just now when I couldn't breathe. And by some kind of epic mistake, I ended up in heaven. Or I passed out and this is all a hugely inappropriate dream. By the time I wake up from this fantasy, the shame will be too much to bear.

She straightens herself and wipes the tears off my face.

"Food's getting cold. Let me serve you."

Even though I've cum already seconds earlier, my cock twitches again when she turns around sideways in my lap.

I want to argue more, but I don't have the energy. All I can do is try not to stare at the way her buttocks curve generously outwards from her lower back when she gets up off me. My God, she's hot. I don't deserve her.

"Okay," I hear myself say in a raspy voice.

She leans over and fixes me a plate of roast turkey with all the trimmings. It all smells amazing. As upset as I was moments earlier, the food distracts me; soothes me, as it usually does.

I realise now how hungry I've been. For Paige's cooking, as well as her attention.

Paige:

That escalated quickly. I hand Eric the plate and watch as he takes his first bite.

He's a basket case alright. But the big difference between him and previous fucked up men I've been with is that he's self-aware and brutally honest about it. I know I can't fix him, not completely. That sort of thing only happens in fairy tales, but I'm hopelessly attracted to him anyway. Maybe, showing him just how much I want him will do wonders for his self-esteem? If it's mostly loneliness he suffers from, perhaps that's one ailment I can actually cure?

Although this affair will probably end in disaster - they usually do- I'm helpless to stop it now. Like a moth to a flame, I'm drawn to him. My cunt aches for him; more so now as I watch him eat.

I know exactly what I want to happen next.

Initially, I'd wanted to show him some kindness. No strings attached. I wanted to show him that I care, and maybe try to be friends at first. Anything, just to have an excuse to spend more time with him going forward. Of course, sex was always the end game. It was always the ultimate goal.

But when I found myself so close to him, something snapped. I realised that I couldn't possibly hold back that long. Patience isn't one of my strengths. Luckily, he seems rather easy to seduce.

First, I want to watch him finish all this food. And then, once he's done, I want to ride him on the sofa. I want to feel his greasy hot lips all over my body. His hands eagerly roaming my naked flesh while I milk his cock for every last drop of cum he's got left to give.

I know he's starved for affection; as am I.

What sort of a guy ejaculates two minutes into a French kiss? Apparently, the sort of guy who calls a hooker once a month, and then doesn't even screw her.

Are his hang ups really so major that he hasn't allowed himself any release even when paying good money for it? Not even once? Or has he been pretending all this time that he's above all that. That he doesn't need the same release the rest of us do? He ain't fooling me, that's for sure. I see the man in him; I see the raw passion hidden underneath that overgrown body of his, just waiting to break free.

Has he ever done it at all, I wonder? Maybe inexperience is the reason he's been so shy with that girl. Clearly, all the plumbing works just fine, so I intend to take it from him before the evening is over.

He cleans his plate, and I top it up. His eyes are fixated on me, but the moment I hand the food to him, he hesitates, as though he wants to say something.

"I don't remember the last time I had a home cooked meal," he mumbles at last.

"You can have a different home cooked meal every day if you want," I counter.

The way he stares at me is everything. I know I've already won.

He tries to put the plate down, but he's sunk too far back into the sofa to be able to reach the coffee table, plus I'm still in his way.

"Done already?" I ask sweetly. 'Yes' is not an answer I'm willing to accept right now. Even I could eat more than this.

He looks up at me, then at the food, and slowly shakes his head.

"Then?" I take the plate from him.

"Something to drink, maybe?" he whispers.

I smile and nod.

Some people just love to serve. I'm one of them. My

blog gives me a little bit of that same satisfaction; to know that my recipes please people. But that's no real replacement for being with someone up close and personal.

And now that I've got Eric exactly where I want, he's a most beautiful and willing subject.

I grab a bottle of coke from the fridge and hand it to him. Although it's a big one, he finishes off nearly a quarter of it in one generous gulp. I lower myself onto his lap again, with the large dinner plate between us.

He sighs and leans into the plush cushions at the back, allowing me to take over. I feed him forkful after forkful of food. All he has to do is chew and swallow. Although he looks uncomfortable with this new dynamic at first, that soon passes. His mind seems to stop racing so much, the more of it he eats. The doubts in his eyes start to fade as he surrenders to my care.

Every so often, I hand him the bottle, and watch as he drinks more and more of the sugary soda. Are my eyes deceiving me or is his belly starting to grow bigger and tauter already?

The hoodie that he'd sneakily zipped back up while I was refilling his plate had started off rather loose. But now, his growing body is straining against it more and more. The t-shirt underneath was already tight as anything earlier. I would love to see the effect all this food is having on it now. I don't know why that turns me on, but I'm starting to soak through my panties just thinking about it.

Underneath me, something else is growing again as

well. I shift my weight just slightly and smile when I feel that same unmistakeable bulge pressing up into me right where it matters. He groans and tightly grips my thigh.

"You like that, huh?" I whisper.

His eyes open again; his breaths quicken through slightly parted lips. I stuff a loaded fork right into his mouth before he can say another word.

Eric:

She's too much. This whole situation is too much.

Just when I think I can fight my way past the sensory overload her food and company provide, my body reacts with even more intensity and I'm hopelessly lost again.

I'm used to overeating; it's what I do. But she seems intent on pushing me to the next level. We're at the third serving and she's been piling the plate high each time. My stomach strains uncomfortably against the confines of my formerly loose sweatshirt. She hands me the bottle of coke, and I finish it off.

I'm so utterly stuffed, I can hardly breathe anymore. Normally I would have stopped a while ago, but I can't say no to her. Her hands massage my bloated belly - I should be horrified to have her touch me in this condition, but my thoughts are too hazy to care anymore. I'm too drunk off of her food.

Just why she wants to do this to me, I have no idea. But I'm beginning to love it.

Every bite she's fed me so far has added to the

eroticism of the moment. This has got to be the sexiest thing I've ever experienced by far. No fantasy; no wet dream could compare to how I feel right now, with Paige continuing to sit in my lap, depositing the last remnants of food from the plate into my mouth.

Obviously, I don't have much sexual experience at all. An early, failed attempt with Leslie's predecessor hardly counts. It was the very first time I ever called a girl over and I was so incredibly anxious about finally getting laid, that I tried to calm myself down with copious amounts of booze. The end result was that I couldn't even get it up, no matter how hard she worked for it. Nothing happened at all, and I was so ashamed, I never dared to call her again.

But with Paige… I'm not even trying; I'm not even *thinking* about trying anything, and my cock is reacting with a mind of its own.

I shouldn't be here. She should have never let me in. There's no way I'll be able to cage the monster she's unleashed inside of me. By now I can't stop myself from holding onto her upper thigh, and keeping her firmly in place in my lap with her ass pressing down on my growing erection.

How is it that I'm hard again? Just half an hour after the first time?

I've sought refuge in food for as long as I can remember, but it never made me feel good like this. I tend to binge to silence my racing thoughts, and then feel worse about myself, which then makes me binge some more. But the way she's admiring me now has stopped the flow of never-ending worries and doubts that usually play on my mind. And I've barely even had a drink today.

Now that the dinner is finished, I can finally look her in the eye and actually see what should have been evident right from the start.

She's as invested in the moment as I am. Every forkful that entered my mouth so far has heightened her excitement. Just what the attraction is for her, I really can't say. But it's such a turn-on to see her like this, I couldn't bear the thought of disappointing her.

"You like to watch me eat," I remark.

She smiles coyly. "Busted."

"This was amazing, by the way. You're a great cook."

Is that a blush on her cheeks I see? "Thanks. It's all for you."

I try not to focus on the subtext in her words. Is it really *all* for me? Is this really the moment I've been waiting for? None of this is happening how I thought it would. It's so much better than anything my imagination could have conjured up.

"You're not hungry?" I ask. "I probably should have asked before finishing everything."

She licks her lips and stares down at my growing belly. "Not for food, I'm not."

My cock squirms underneath her. I'm helplessly stuck. Weighed down not just by the limitations of my broken body, but also the insane amount of turkey and mashed potato she's managed to cram into me. But I'm not worried about it anymore. The lust in her eyes isn't giving me any room for doubt. She truly wants me here. It's a new feeling for me; to be desired. A new form of addiction I could get used to.

"For dessert?" I suggest.

She glances at what I'm assuming is the kitchen door behind me. "I have a few options to choose from in the fridge."

I try to take a deep breath. My stomach is so full, my lungs are painfully constrained against my insides. I exhale and am a little shocked by how laboured it sounds.

"Not what I meant," I whisper, while glancing down at the full cleavage, as yet hidden underneath her sweater.

Again, no idea where this sudden courage is coming from. A part of me is expecting a tight slap just to put me back in my place again.

She bites her lip and smiles. "Oh, *that* kind of dessert! Always."

Just like that, she grinds her ass into my crotch again. I could cum all over again if I'm not careful. My fingers dig into her thigh and I let out a deep groan.

Why does she want this? Why has she chosen me? How do I make sure I don't disappoint her, after everything she's done for me already? I'm so full, I feel like I'm going to burst, but my cock is again aching for release underneath that sexy, firm ass of hers. Hardly any time has passed since I prematurely jizzed myself during our first kiss, and yet I've never been this horny in my entire life.

Paige:

He's starting to show a bit of attitude. I love it.

He's emptied his plate again and with it, all the containers I'd carried here from the kitchen. I discard the plate and cutlery on the sofa beside us. Both my arms find their way around his neck again and I look down to admire my prize for the night.

Hungry eyes meet mine. I lean down and taste his lips, licking off the little droplet of gravy left in the corner of his mouth.

He squirms underneath me and carries on panting for air.

"You're gorgeous, Paige. I don't deserve you," he tells me in between laboured breaths.

I try to take his hand. He's so tense I almost have to pry his fingers off my thigh before being able to relocate it to my chest. He gently cups my breast and my heart races even faster. I'm so pleased I decided to wear an unpadded bra today, just to make the most of this moment. The only way his touch would feel better is if it were skin on skin. We'll get there, soon.

"Tonight is going to be a night to remember," I say.

"It already is. A dream that couldn't possibly come true."

"And yet it has."

I've been dreaming about this too. Maybe not exactly this; feeding him to the point of stuffing his huge belly beyond its former limits kind of happened in the heat of the moment. But overall, I've fantasised about his big sexy body so much, it's been keeping me awake most nights.

"I don't want to disappoint you," he says.

"You couldn't possibly." I slip my hand underneath his t-shirt and massage his hard, swollen belly to make my point. I know exactly what I want from him. Everything.

He tries to look down at what I'm doing, but it's obvious that it's physically difficult for him to see much of anything down there. His eyes are growing heavy; he's obviously enjoying my touch as much as I am.

"You could literally go out there and take a different man home every night if you wanted," he whispers.

I smile and shake my head. "I want *you*, though. No one else."

"Someone handsome and desirable; someone who can treat you like the goddess you are."

His words affect me deeply; making me even wetter than I already was. How did shy Eric turn into such a charmer all of a sudden?

"If that's how you feel about me, then I'm certain you'll work hard to satisfy my every need," I whisper.

His eyes soften when he looks up at me again. "I'll try my best."

I know you will, baby.

"Undress me," I say.

My demand seems to shock him. His hand freezes on my tit.

"Don't you want to see?" I ask.

"God, yes," he stammers.

I lean down and grab his bottom lip with my teeth, tugging at it gently. I could just eat him up. His short gasps for air tickle against my face. He's so stuffed, I wonder if he's ever felt like this before. I wonder if overeating normally turns him on too or if this is a new discovery for him. Because there's no doubt in my mind that he's gagging for it as much as I am by now. He'll make a beautiful subject for me going forward. His capacity for eating is already huge, but I'm sure we can stretch his limits even further together. He'll be the perfect feedee for me. A dream come true.

"Do it, then," I say. "Inspect the goods."

His fingers tremble as he reaches for my sweater and slides it upwards. The cool air tickles against my bare skin, sending goose bumps up and down my spine.

He pulls it all the way up and over my head. My pink lace bra is revealed. Locks of hair cascade down my shoulders, tickling me along the way.

I raise myself off him slightly.

"Bottoms too," I say.

He inhales sharply as he hooks his fingers into my waistband and slips my pyjamas down over my round buttocks and generous hips. In his eagerness he's taken my panties down too, but I don't mind. That's where things were headed anyway.

I reach behind my back and unhook my bra for him, studying his reaction all the while. He looks about ready to cum for me again. But this time I won't let him waste it; no way.

This time, I want to feel it gushing into me, where it

belongs.

"Your turn," I whisper, tugging at the sleeve of his hoodie. "I want everything off."

It was already unzipped, but getting it off his shoulders and arms takes some effort from both of us. Our little feeding session didn't help any; his full, proud belly is restricting his movements quite a bit further.

But once I get up and he turns slightly onto one side, we manage to get the sweatshirt and stretched out t-shirt off him at last.

He's even sexier than I could have imagined. Vast and glorious is the canvas that is his giant body. His belly is tight and hard and much bigger than earlier, before dinner. I run my hand across his hairy chest.

"You're such a manly man, aren't you?" I squeal. "I love it."

He shyly looks up at me. The wonder in his eyes is addictive.

Eric:

I'm half-naked in front of Paige, and I'm not even drunk. How the hell did things happen so quickly?

Ever since our dynamic changed, I've been wavering between almost exploding into my shorts again, and threatening to lose my erection to shame. Neither is a good option, when it's so obvious she expects me to perform for her.

She doesn't know just how pathetic I am. How inexperienced.

She doesn't even seem to realise just how ugly I am either. The more of me comes into view, the more intense the lust in her eyes becomes. And this is me at my worst. At my ugliest. At my fattest, ever. She made it happen just now with all the food she's fed me, and she looks pretty damn pleased about it too.

"Pants off," she orders, while getting up off me and stepping out of her own pyjamas.

I pause for a moment and take in the view of her naked body. Perky boobs accentuate the slender waist sitting above perfectly rounded hips and long, toned legs. The fact that she hasn't shaved her armpits or her pubes actually makes the image even more perfect than any porn clip could be. Because it isn't staged or planned. This is *real*. I can't believe it's happening to me. I've done nothing to deserve this, but she doesn't seem to share these reservations.

If this were any other place; and any other girl, I would have expected it to be a set-up. A part of me is waiting for the camera crew and laughter track. *Psych! What made you think she actually wants you? What a loser!*

But that doesn't happen, of course. She's stuffed me like a pig for her own enjoyment, and now she wants her efforts to pay off.

In front of me stands a vision of perfection, impatiently waiting for me to surrender what's left of my modesty to her. How can I refuse, after everything she's done for me? After showing me kindness as well as passion I've never known before? I owe it to her to give her anything--everything-- she wants.

As sharp as the ache in my knees when I lift my hips upwards is, I don't let it stop me. I grit my teeth and fight through it, wiggling my jeans and also my boxer shorts off me, taking the incriminating evidence of my earlier release along with it.

She lets out a gasp and my heart sinks. But when I glance up to see her expression, I realise it wasn't horror that caused her little outburst. She grins at me as she leans down and wraps her elegant fingers around my unworthy cock. I do all I can to keep calm, but I'm shivering uncontrollably anyway. Deep breath, hold, release, just like she instructed me earlier. It helps, but only slightly.

It wouldn't take anything for me to cum again. At this rate, she'll have me gushing like a volcano within seconds.

"Your cock is so big and fat too. I love it," she remarks. "But you're going to have to move back further to give me room."

She firmly grips my shaft; stroking it a couple of times and really working to get down to the base which is hidden underneath my big belly. I wish I could see, though if I could, the view would probably horrify me. Instead, I focus on the sensation of everything she's doing.

Guided by her left hand on my chest, I wiggle over to the side and lay down flat on the sofa. Just how I'm ever going to get up from here, I have no idea. But I have no choice. Heaven is just within reach.

She gets on top, spreading her sexy toned thighs

across my lap and settling down just with the tip of my dick pressing into what I'm assuming must be her crotch.

What the hell do I do now? I can't even move like this!

"I'm a virgin," I blurt out, then try miserably to catch my breath when a fresh wave of anxiety hits. "I've never done anything like this before."

She lowers herself onto me. The feeling of her moist cunt fusing with my cock sends me panting like a dog all over again. Short, shallow, desperate breaths that fail to satisfy my need for oxygen. All this food, weighing down on me, leaves hardly any room for my lungs to fill up. My whole body is primed to burst; I'm going to cum harder and faster than I ever have in my entire life.

"Actually, you're not. Not anymore."

She cups my face and kisses me slowly while starting to move on top of me. I can't even describe what that does to me. I could laugh. I could cry. I could scream. None seem appropriate, so I just keep quiet and close my eyes.

I couldn't see a damn thing of what's happening down there anyway. It's been well over a decade since I've seen my dick without the help of a mirror. So instead I continue to focus on what it feels like and imagine the rest. In and out it moves. Gently, deeply, beautifully. My hands find the widest part of her hips and I start to follow her rhythm. Her soft little stomach brushes against my painfully bloated belly with every move.

She moans into my mouth. "So good. Just as I'd hoped."

Her fingers twitch on my neck as she starts to smother me with further kisses. I don't even care that she's making it even harder for me to breathe by leaning on me. If I died right now, I'd die the happiest man in the world.

She isn't faking, is she? Why would she be, when there's nobody else here watching the show? Everything I witness is just for me, bizarre as it seems.

Her slow yet deliberate movements threaten to drive me crazy. I can't stop myself from moaning loudly every time she grinds down into my sticky, sweaty crotch.

I start to explore her exquisite body with my hands; caressing the contours of her back, the sharp dip at the smallest part of her waist… I cup one hand over her naked breast and enjoy how her hard nipple grazes my palm with every move of hers. That little jiggle in her flesh, it's so tiny compared to mine and yet it's the most beautiful thing ever. I can feel her ribs, her muscles, working away underneath my fingertips. So, this is what perfection feels like; it's overwhelming and brings fresh tears to my eyes. She appears so small and fragile, and yet I know she's stronger than me in so many ways.

Despite the horrendous contrast between us physically, it's a perfect moment. Much awaited and always out of reach, until tonight.

This might have happened with the girl I'd hired before Leslie, but I'm glad now that it didn't materialise. I was so bloody wasted; I didn't even feel anything, except the lingering shame. It was dirty and abusive. She didn't want to be there either; she just wanted to get paid.

With Paige, I feel things I've never known. Even at times when I've rubbed one out on my own. I've felt ashamed. Even without an audience; without anyone there to judge me, I felt like I didn't deserve to feel good about it. But in this moment, I try to let go of all that and allow myself to enjoy all these things I'm feeling. Her initiation gave me permission to do so, strangely enough.

Paige wants me, at least for now. She's using me for her own pleasure first and I don't even know why. I can clearly see the need in her eyes whenever her lids do open to look down on me. I feel the purpose in her movements. The excitement with which she touches my naked flesh. She knows I'm hers; unconditionally, because she's reached out and plucked me from the dirt just to claim me.

"You feel so big inside of me," she moans. "Oh, I've dreamed of this so many times!"

Her words are enough to send me over the edge of control.

I shudder against the sofa; both my hands dig into her hips and force her down hard. She's taking all I have to offer; my whole cock is balls deep inside of her when I explode.

"Oh yeah, baby, fill me up!" she cries out.

Despite my firm grip on her, she wiggles free and continues to grind into me, harder, faster, a couple more times.

"Oh fuck, I'm gonna cum!" she screams.

My mind is blank; my eyes shut involuntarily. She slams down one last time against my spent cock, and her whole body goes rigid. Her fingernails run all the way down my chest and belly before she freezes, save for a slight shiver that passes through her core.

Our combined sweat stings the wounds she leaves on my torso. But I don't care. I'll wear these red scars with pride and hope they never fade. They'll remind me of that time when Paige let me into her flat and made me worthy. The long overdue moment when I accidentally became a man.

She sinks down against my chest; her lithe body drapes itself over my round, bloated belly, making it almost impossible for me to breathe. Long locks of hair tickle as they stick to my damp skin. I wouldn't have it any other way.

I wrap my arms around her and just hold her. I can't believe it. Here I thought she was taking care of me, indulging me, but I've actually managed to give her something in return. It was my first time ever, and as such I still have no idea what I'm supposed to be doing. Still, she didn't just enjoy herself; she came right along with me. I did that. *My cock* did that for her.

A warmth fills my chest which I'm unaccustomed to. Pride? Contentment?

I defiled her body; dirtied it with my sweat and my semen, but she's pure and perfect as ever. A sexy naked angel in my arms. Come down from heaven to save me from the emptiness of my existence.

I don't know what comes over me. In this amazingly surreal moment, I find the courage to hold her tight and kiss her damp hair before pressing my face into it. This post-orgasmic bliss almost convinces me she's mine to keep, as unrealistic as that is.

Her hand stirs on my chest, playing with the short curls gracing the centre of my chest, before moving on to fondling and squeezing my man-tit. It should be weird, embarrassing, but it's nice instead. I can't help but smile as she continues to pet my furry body while trying to catch her breath.

She's the first and only person I've ever shown myself to; at least in my adult life. And she hasn't judged me, when all I've done for years on end is hate this body of mine. Her touch is effortless. Without hesitation or disgust; even those parts which horrify me. And she's doing it because it brings *her* joy.

For once in my life, I have so much to say. So many emotions to express that aren't based in fear. It's impossible to put it all into words, so instead, I continue to caress her naked, spent body. I worship her with my hands as best I can, even if the pressure her little frame is putting on my overly stretched belly is making it so hard for me to breathe. I don't care. I would happily die tonight if only it was in her arms.

This wasn't even the end game for me, and yet I feel like I've reached my potential in life. I'm done. Everything that happens now is gravy.

Our breaths slow and she stirs slightly in my arms,

reminding me that my cock is still buried deep inside her. She allowed me to cum in her without a condom. Why?

She's continuing to let me touch her, kiss her, cuddle with her. To what end?

Earlier she said she was crushing on me. Then, moments later, she fed me ungodly amounts of food, all to further her own pleasure. How bizarre. It hadn't even occurred to me that she'd noticed me too.

Of course, I spotted her the day she moved into this flat. Her presence did something to me which I couldn't understand. Like an absolute freak, I would time my infrequent outings to moments when I heard activity at her place as well. Like a shadow, I tried to remain close to my subject, so that I might catch a glimpse of her; even exchange a few words which I would then analyse to death afterwards over copious amounts of alcohol.

I thought she wouldn't notice. That she would accept our awkward meetings as coincidence and then forget about me once we went our separate ways. Thinking back, it surprises me that she never even tried to avoid me either.

I'm slow and clumsy at the best of times, but I wasn't at my best when I interacted with her previously. Mostly, I was varying shades of drunk, like I generally am. The best excuse I could come up with to go out and *accidentally* bump into her was to go to the off-license next door. It's the furthest I've ventured from home in ages and I did it only so I could spend a few seconds in the lift with her along the way.

Any sane person would have cut a wide berth around me. If she'd been cautious, she could have very well avoided me after the first few times. She could have changed her routine. She could have let the doors close on me so many times, pretending not to hear or see me coming.

She could have done a lot of things…

But instead, she always held the lift and waited with a smile on her face. Because she'd noticed me too.

"Why don't I put you off?" I wonder aloud. "Why want any of this?"

She sighs lazily. "Because…"

This is the moment when she tells me she doesn't want it at all. Maybe she was just horny and alone, and I've served my purpose now. She'll tell me any moment now that this was all a big lapse in judgement on her part and to forget it ever happened.

"Because I like you."

Not the answer I was expecting. "You don't know me. Not really."

"I know what I've seen in your eyes."

Now that the urgency of the moment has waned somewhat, I try to think back to everything she's already said to me. Most of it seems so unlikely, I'm almost certain I must have imagined it. Like when she told me earlier that she likes how I look. Impossible.

"You don't believe me, do you?" She lifts her head and looks down at me.

"I'm not even entirely convinced this is really happening," I say.

She smiles and my heart is aflutter. I don't recall ever *feeling* anything so intensely. Except the existential dread that follows me around most days. I tend to feel that pretty deeply just before I start drinking in the mornings.

"Same," she says. "I didn't think you were interested."

Me? Not interested? I've been following her around like a hugely overgrown, socially awkward puppy.

"So, my efforts to stalk you haven't been too obvious, then?" I ask.

She lets out a laugh. The bright sound of her voice tickles the centre of my chest and I can't help but grin widely as a result.

"Have you been? Stalking me, I mean?" She runs her fingers through my hair while studying my eyes. I want to kiss her again. And again. But I dare not, just in case I'm overstepping some boundary I'm as yet unaware of. She's still on top; still in control.

"By the way, I love your smile. You should smile more often," she adds, while running her fingertip across the corner of my mouth.

"I've followed you every single time I left the house ever since you moved in."

"Liar. You've been going to the shops. Or putting the garbage out."

Part of me is still shocked that she noticed those things. My badly thought out 'excuses'.

"I get my groceries delivered," I explain, but then realise that doesn't really explain anything. I'm not like other people. Not normal, like her. "I normally don't go out at all."

"Why?"

As obvious as her question is, I'm not sure how to answer it without sounding pathetic. *Because people would judge me? Because I'm terrified I'll be in so much pain after walking a little, I won't make it back home again and there won't be anyone there to help me?* There are a thousand reasons and I can't bear to tell her even one.

"I don't know," I mumble.

"I'm glad you made an exception for me today. Because I really needed this."

Again, her responses puzzle me. She's pretending like I did *her* a favour by coming over here, eating all her food, sweating into her sofa and getting laid for the first time ever. I must be dreaming.

In spite of everything I continue to keep from her, I feel lighter in my chest. The dark cloud that has been following me around for most of my life isn't pressing down quite so hard on me right now.

"Impossible." I sigh.

"Is it because of the anxiety attacks?" she asks, while planting soft kisses on the side of my neck. It tickles, but in a nice way. "Is that why you don't go out?"

"Yeah." That, and everything else I'm too afraid to tell her about.

"I've been really nervous around you, or I might have asked you over sooner." She sighs. "If I had known..."

Be still my aching heart. "You have nothing to be

nervous about, Paige. Every time you spoke to me in the lift, I was so terrified, I wanted to just vanish."

She leans back and looks at me with a worried frown on her face. "I didn't want to make you uncomfortable! I just wanted to get to know you."

I quickly shake my head. *Shit, now I've made her feel bad.* "You didn't. I make myself uncomfortable."

"Okay, well, if you try to stop torturing yourself, then I'll try to stop being nervous around you too," she says.

The way she's looking into my eyes now flips a switch in me. I reach for her beautiful face and guide it down towards me, pressing my lips into hers for that kiss I've been craving so much.

Part of me expects her to withdraw, but she doesn't. She opens herself up to me. She wraps her arms around me so tightly, the gesture tries to wipe the last shred of doubt from my heart.

A million butterflies flood in my stomach until even the centre of my chest starts to tickle, making me want to scream her name loud enough for the whole world to hear. I don't, of course. Instead, I whisper it.

"Paige." *I think I love you...*

Paige:

I can't believe how beautifully all of this turned out. Eric claims he's been stalking me, which doesn't make a whole lot of sense, because I always thought *I* was the one creeping on *him*. But he'd have no reason to lie.

So that means, every time we met. Every time I've held the elevator doors, hoping for him to catch up with me, our meetings were orchestrated by him too. They weren't the little coincidences I thought they were.

As though he could feel my attraction. He instinctively knew we were meant to interact, no matter how awkward it made him feel. We were supposed to get to know one another little by little during those half a dozen short meetings which led us to this point.

"I don't want to let you go," I whisper, with my arms still wrapped around his neck.

"Same here." His voice sounds choked.

I rest one hand on his cheek. It's so wonderfully chubby, so soft despite the stubble he's sporting today. I can't get enough of how squishy he feels all over.

"Paige," he speaks up again.

I pull back and look into his eyes again.

"Yes?"

"I'm not like other people," he says. "I've never had anyone who cared."

"I care," I say. I do. So deeply, I hardly know what to do with myself. It doesn't make sense, but emotions rarely do. Is this what love feels like? I wouldn't know, because I've never felt this way before.

He shakes his head. "It's not fair on you. I'm broken."

"You've been going through a tough time," I say. "That's hardly a crime."

He sighs and closes his eyes again. I rest my forehead against his cheek and listen to his strained breaths. The world can be a cold and cruel place to be, but everything between us feels right. Like today was meant to turn out like this to teach us important truths we could have not learned otherwise.

I know there is a lot he's not saying. A lot of stuff he's dealing with that he isn't comfortable sharing with me yet. But that's okay. This is only the first chapter of a new beginning for the two of us. Eric and me. Neighbours as well as lovers, just trying to figure all of this out for the very first time.

"Thank you," he says.

"For?"

"I guess, for existing."

I smile and carry on running my fingers through his chest hair, before kissing him there and cuddling my face in it.

He feels so good against my bare skin. So perfect. He's everything I want and it appears that the feeling is definitely mutual.

I'll spend every waking moment trying to convince him of what I've figured out here, lying naked in his arms. There's a reason I'm attracted to broken men; tortured heroes. This is what I'm meant to do. Here is where I feel at home.

I will love him for as long as he continues to want me. I'll accept him, flawed as he is, and work tirelessly to build him up again whenever he feels down. I'll feed him when he wants to be fed; hopefully often. I'll pleasure him as many times as he needs to feel like the man I know him to be. I'll massage his aching muscles afterwards, and care for him in any way he requires.

I'll do whatever he wants, whenever he needs it. This is my new mission. And I'm prepared to follow through on it.

And all I want in return is this. His arms, shielding me from the cool air of my apartment. His hands, caressing me softly, because he *wants* to, not because he has to. His thick cock buried deep inside of me at a moment's notice. For his body and soul to exclusively mine, simply because I know he's too damn shy to go around with any other girl.

"Running into you in the hallway was always the highlight of my day," I mumble.

"Mine too."

"But I won't have to do that anymore now, will I?"

"I guess not." He clears his throat.

"I'll just knock on your door instead."

"Any time." His arms twitch around me.

"Careful what you wish for. Because I'll want to do it all of the time."

As soon as I finish my sentence, Eric groans softly and digs his fingers into my back. Just like that. Just minutes after shooting a huge load into me, his cock stirs a little until I can feel it poking into my lower abdomen.

"Ready to go again?" I whisper in his ear, nibbling softly on his earlobe.

The way his breathing changes, tells me all I need to know. It makes me smile. He has a lot of catching up to do. And I'm all too willing to play along.

"Maybe this time you wanna cum in my mouth?" I ask, while grinding my hips into him.

This time, my words elicit a desperate moan and a full-body shudder.

"Yeah, I thought so…" I say, while slowly getting up off of him and kneeling down on the carpet beside the couch.

I run my hands across his big torso, making sure to appreciate every little fold and dimple in his luxurious flesh, before getting to his fat thighs and spreading them apart to give me access.

"You don't have to-" he whispers, but I silence his doubts quickly by putting his cock in my mouth. "Oh God!"

I know I don't have to. But fuck, do I want to. So, I start sucking. Slowly, deeply, full of determination. And he's done for. Moaning and panting, out of control all over again.

It's beautiful. *He's* beautiful. I wish I could tell him, but that will have to wait.

All I can do is show him.

I mouthfuck him deeply. Faster, then slower. Teasing the moment, stretching it out and maximising his pleasure as best as I can.

And he responds eagerly with every stroke. His hand reaches down and finds my hair, which he fists only momentarily. Then he lets go and finds my hand on his belly instead, threading his fingers through mine as if to say he's surrendered.

He's mine. I am his.

I speed up, bobbing up and down on his cock at a steady pace now. We're almost there. We've almost arrived at nirvana.

And once we do, we're going to do this all over again.

ABOUT THE AUTHOR

Dear Reader,

If you came across me in real life, you'd never guess the kind of filth I like to read and write. Cleverly disguised as a boring office worker, the drudgery of my 9-to-5 only because bearable because of my vivid and explicit imagination. I like fat guys and I cannot lie. In my world, bigger (fatter) is always better. It's been that way for as long as I can remember.

Thanks for reading this story, one of hopefully many of my published sexual fantasies. My stories revolve around one common theme: really big men and the women who can't help but lust for them.

Although I like porn just fine, it's nearly impossible to find it in the flavour that I desire. The written word allows me to explore a world of lush excess that mainstream adult entertainment just cannot provide. When I started writing, I soon discovered the beauty of having a catalog of erotica out there to satisfy my own lustful needs. This is a passion project more than a money-grab.

So, first and foremost, my writing is for me. But perhaps there are other women (or even men) out there who share my tastes; my fetishes and fantasies? My fascination with the larger male form, and sexualisation of food (especially overeating). If that sounds like something you'll wank off to, you've come to the right place.

xxx Hedonist

To find out more, check:

 ❖ eXplicitTales.com

www.ingramcontent.com/pod-product-compliance
Lightning Source LLC
Chambersburg PA
CBHW070512170726
48291CB00008B/2718